A Valentine for Fuzzboom

TRUE KELLEY

Houghton Mifflin Company   Boston   1981

For steven Lindblom

Library of Congress Cataloging in Publication Data

Kelley, True
    A valentine for Fuzzboom.

    SUMMARY: Lima Bean, a lovesick young rabbit, gets
up the nerve to send her idol, Fuzzboom, a valentine.
    [1. Rabbits—Fiction. 2. St. Valentine's Day—Fic-
tion] I. Title.
PZ7.K2824Val   [E]   80-24284
ISBN 0-395-30446-6

Printed in the United States of America.

Y   10 9 8 7 6 5 4 3 2 1

Lima Bean was madly in love with Fuzzboom.
Lima's best friend Grilby thought she was
being yucky and mushy. But Lima couldn't
help it.

The first time Lima saw Fuzzboom was in Farmer Dillgood's garden. Lima had eaten halfway down a row of carrots. Fuzzboom had eaten the other half, and they met in the middle. It was love at first sight for Lima. Fuzzboom was annoyed that Lima had eaten the other half·of his row.

When Farmer Dillgood came out to chase them
away, Fuzzboom quickly uprooted a huge
radish and escaped with his mouth full. Lima
thought this was very dashing.
Grilby said it was greedy.

That was how it began. Lima Bean had a hopeless crush on Fuzzboom. Grilby said he wasn't worth it. Grilby thought there were lots of nicer rabbits around. But Lima thought Fuzzboom was IT! The Cat's Pajamas!

Lima Bean thought about Fuzzboom all the
time. His face would appear in her beet soup at
breakfast. Grilby said he had a face like a
mashed beet.

Clouds reminded Lima of him. Grilby said
Fuzzboom was a lightweight and a cloud-brain.
Whenever Lima ran into Fuzzboom, she felt
giggly all over. Fuzzboom always ignored her.
Grilby said he was too stuck up to notice
anyone but himself.

Lima Bean was so lovesick she misplaced
things.
She lost one roller skate. And both of her
orange mittens.

She became forgetful.

She forgot Grilby's birthday.

"Enough is enough," Grilby said. "Why don't you make him a valentine, and see what happens? Then maybe you'll find out what a jerk he is!"

Lima Bean thought that was an excellent idea, even if it was only October.

She went down to the store and bought lots of crayons and paper.

Every day she made Fuzzboom a valentine.

She couldn't decide which one to send him,
so she kept on making more. She kept them
all under her pillow. On the day before
Valentine's Day, Lima Bean had 127
valentines.

"You'd better send just one, for now," advised Grilby.

Lima Bean spent all day narrowing it down to the best one.

Some were too silly.

Some were too mushy.

Some were too pushy.

Finally, Lima Bean settled on one.

It said:

Lettuce be Valentines

Love, Lima Bean

Lima Bean put it in the mailbox with shaking paws.

Lima couldn't sleep all night. She wondered if she had sent the right valentine. She worried that Fuzzboom would laugh or get mad. All Valentine's Day she waited.

Grilby made valentine cookies, but Lima
couldn't touch them.

Grilby gave Lima a funny valentine card, but
Lima didn't even smile.

Lima Bean waited all the next day and the
next. Still there was no answer from Fuzzboom.
"The least he could do is say thank you," said
Grilby. "I told you he wasn't worth it."
Lima cried herself to sleep.

After a whole week, Lima said to Grilby, "I think you're right. He must be a jerk not even to answer me. I'm sorry I forgot your birthday and didn't eat your valentine cookies and didn't laugh at your funny valentine. You're a good friend to put up with me, and I want you to have all 126 of my leftover valentines." "Thank you, Lima. You are very nice when you're not being dumb," said Grilby.

"I'm going to go to Fuzzboom's house and tell him what I think of him. Then I'll come home and have stale valentine cookies and tea with you," said Lima.

Fuzzboom answered the angry furry-fisted
knock at his door.

"You are mean not even to answer my valentine," said Lima Bean. "You are a stuck-up cloud-brain, and your face looks like a squashed beet, and I hope you never treat another rabbit the way you treated me!"

"Hey, I like a rabbit with spirit," said Fuzzboom coolly. "I like the way your ears whip around in the air when you're mad. How's about being my valentine?"

And you know what Lima Bean said?